I would like to thank my husband, Ehud Nathaniel,
who has always encouraged me to follow my dreams;
my Mom, Hemda Brav, who taught me how to rhyme and be
passionate about children's books;
my friends: Odelia, Roni, Michelle, Maria and Sharon who
were there for me at every step of the way;
and last, but definitely not least, my children: Yuval, Omer
and Noga who are (and will always be), my constant
inspiration.
Thank you my little princess, Noga, for loving sparkles!
"Sparkly Me" would not exist without you!

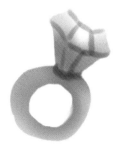

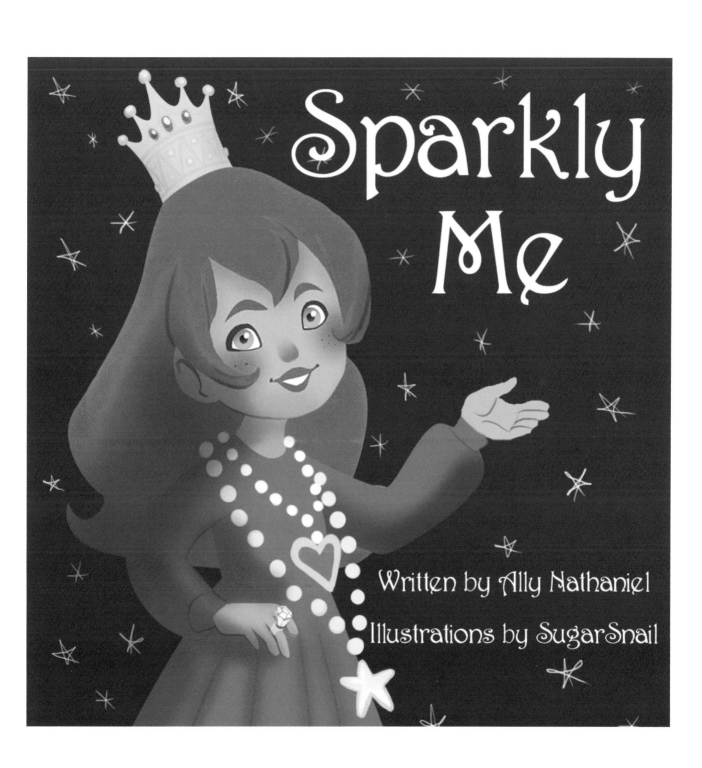

Sparkly Me

Written by Ally Nathaniel

Illustrations by SugarSnail

"I like it," said Emma.
"It's shiny, it's sparkly.

It makes me feel good.
It makes me feel happy

I like it on my feet,
or around my neck.

When I'm inside the house,
or sitting on the deck.

Please give me
the sparkle
when I first wake up.

I'll take it to school and keep it in my backpack.

Sparkles make me
feel good,
sparkles are my style.

That's why I like it
so much,
that's why it makes
me smile.

I will carry it around
keep it close to my heart.

I will hug it so tight.
I will hug it so hard.

Oh, no!

Now my sparkly things
are wrinkled
but that is extra fine.

Because the sparkle
in my heart
is what really makes me
shine".

Other Books by Ally Nathaniel

Quick Order Form

Fax orders: 612-241-4463. Send this form.

Telephone orders: Call 973-826-2020.
Have your credit card ready

@ Email orders: Ally@AllyNathaniel.com

Please sent the following books. I understand that I may return any of them for a full refund-for any reason, no question asked.

_____

_____

_____

Please send more FREE information on:

☐Other Books   ☐ Speaking/Seminars   ☐ Consulting

Name_____

Address_____

City:_____ State:_____ Zip:_____

Telephone_____

Email address_____

sales Tax: Please add 7% sales tax.

Shipping by air: U.S.: $4.00 for first book and $2.00 for each aditional product. International: $9.00 first book; $5.00 for each additional product (estimate).